BATMAN™
RETURNS

The Penguin's Plot

Story adapted by Michael Teitelbaum
Illustrated by Rick Holberg and Tad Chow

A GOLDEN BOOK • NEW YORK
Western Publishing Company, Inc., Racine, Wisconsin 53404

MCMXCIII

It was Christmas in Gotham City. A crowd had gathered in Gotham Plaza for the lighting of the Christmas tree.

The mayor of Gotham City stepped up to the podium to address the holiday crowd.

"Ladies and gentlemen, welcome to our tree-lighting ceremony," he began, when a giant box wrapped like a Christmas present appeared in the street above the plaza.

Suddenly the box flew open and a gang of circus performers rushed into the crowd. There were clowns on motorcycles, stilt walkers, fire eaters, strongmen, and acrobats leaping in the air.

Shrieks of terror rose from the crowd as the performers knocked down everyone in their path.

Police Commissioner Gordon, who was on hand for the ceremony, flipped on his car radio and called headquarters. "What are you waiting for!" he shouted. "Turn on the Bat Signal!"

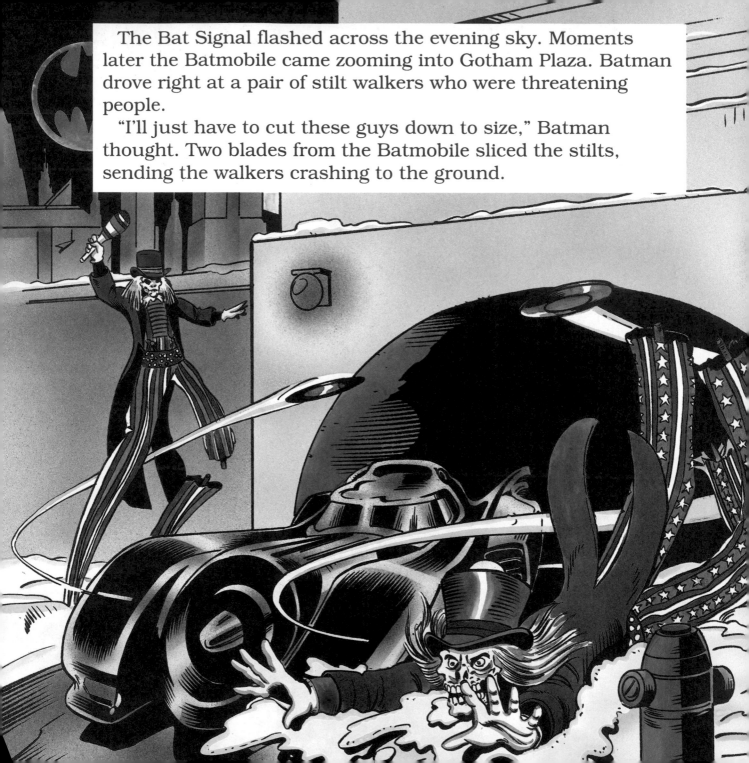

The Bat Signal flashed across the evening sky. Moments later the Batmobile came zooming into Gotham Plaza. Batman drove right at a pair of stilt walkers who were threatening people.

"I'll just have to cut these guys down to size," Batman thought. Two blades from the Batmobile sliced the stilts, sending the walkers crashing to the ground.

  As Batman leapt from the Batmobile, two acrobats came tumbling toward him. He stopped one acrobat with each hand. "Better luck next time, boys!" cried Batman.

  "Who are they, Batman?" asked Commissioner Gordon.

  "The last time I saw them, they were respected performers in the Red Triangle Circus," explained Batman. "But now, it seems, they use their special talents for crime."

  "Let's get out of here!" shouted one of the clowns. "Head for the sewer!"

The Red Triangle Circus Gang hurried through the underground tunnels that led to the abandoned Arctic World Pavilion at the Gotham Park Zoo, which was located above the sewer system. This was The Penguin's hideout.

"The plan is working perfectly," squawked The Penguin to his gang. "Tomorrow we'll take the next step toward making me, Oswald Cobblepot, mayor of Gotham City!"

The next day Gotham City's mayor, with his wife and their baby, toured the damage in the plaza. A television camera crew and the press followed them.

"This eruption of lawlessness will never happen again!" vowed the mayor.

Suddenly an acrobat somersaulted up to the mayor's wife, grabbed her baby, and headed for a manhole.

Seconds later sounds of men fighting came from the manhole—followed by an incredible sight. The Penguin rose slowly out of the manhole, holding the baby!

"I gave that thug a thrashing," said The Penguin, handing the baby back. "Your child, madam."

"Thank you," said the mayor, staring at The Penguin in surprise.

That night Bruce Wayne (who was really Batman) could not believe his eyes as he sat in Wayne Manor, watching the news on television.

"Here is Gotham's newest hero!" announced the newscaster as The Penguin appeared on the screen. "Will he replace Batman in the hearts of Gothamites?"

"The Penguin controls the Red Triangle Circus Gang," Bruce told his faithful butler, Alfred. "I'll bet the baby-snatching was staged to make The Penguin look like a hero. He's up to something big, Alfred. You can bet on it!"

Bruce Wayne could not have been more correct! During the next few weeks, The Penguin sent his Red Triangle Circus Gang on a crime spree in Gotham City. The Penguin was careful to stay out of sight so no one would connect him to the crimes.

The gang blew up automatic teller machines and stole the cash inside. Stores were burglarized and citizens were robbed. No one knew what would happen next—except for Batman!

A few nights later, when the gang arrived to rob a store, Batman was waiting.

"It's Batman! Let's get him!" screamed The Knife Thrower. She tossed a knife at The Dark Knight, who ducked away just in time. Batman quickly programmed his Batarang to bounce from clown to clown, knocking each one out.

But before Batman could retrieve his weapon, a trained circus poodle snatched the Batarang in its teeth, ran from the store, and darted down an open manhole.

The next day in Gotham Plaza, The Penguin announced that he wanted to be mayor of Gotham City.

"Your mayor is helpless against these criminals," said The Penguin. "I say dump him and make me the mayor!"

Everyone cheered. Over the next few days, the citizens of Gotham City began to support the "Cobblepot for Mayor" campaign.

With the election campaign under way, The Penguin now planned to turn the people of Gotham City against the one man who could stop him—Batman!

That night The Penguin kidnapped a beauty queen, known as the Ice Princess, from her dressing room in Gotham Plaza. To complete the frame-up, he left the stolen Batarang behind.

"When the police find the Batarang at the scene of the crime," The Penguin squealed with glee, "Batman will be accused of the kidnapping!"

Back at Wayne Manor, Bruce and Alfred were listening to reports of the kidnapping.

"The Penguin has framed me, Alfred," said Bruce. "I have to show that *he*'s the crook and clear Batman's name. But first I have to rescue the Ice Princess!"

Batman took off in the Batmobile. When he got to Gotham Plaza, he spotted the Ice Princess through a window in a nearby building.

Batman burst into the room and quickly set her free.

"Thanks, Batman!" said the Ice Princess. "Some ugly birdman with fish breath did this to me. I hope you can find him!"

"I'll find him!" replied Batman grimly.

The Penguin had left the Ice Princess in a place where he knew Batman would find her. And while Batman was with the Ice Princess, The Penguin's gang sabotaged the Batmobile. They rigged the vehicle so that it could be operated by remote control!

Batman returned to the Batmobile and started to drive away. Suddenly The Penguin's face appeared on the monitor screen.

"Don't adjust your set," cackled The Penguin. "Hold tight, Batman, and have an unsafe ride!"

Batman was helpless! The Penguin sent the Batmobile on a high-speed, remote-controlled ride through the city.

"It was easy for me to frame you, Batman," squawked The Penguin. As The Penguin spoke, Batman reached down and flipped on the Batmobile's CD recorder. He was taping all of The Penguin's nasty comments!

"And when I'm through with you," The Penguin went on, "I'll take care of the pinhead citizens of Gotham City!

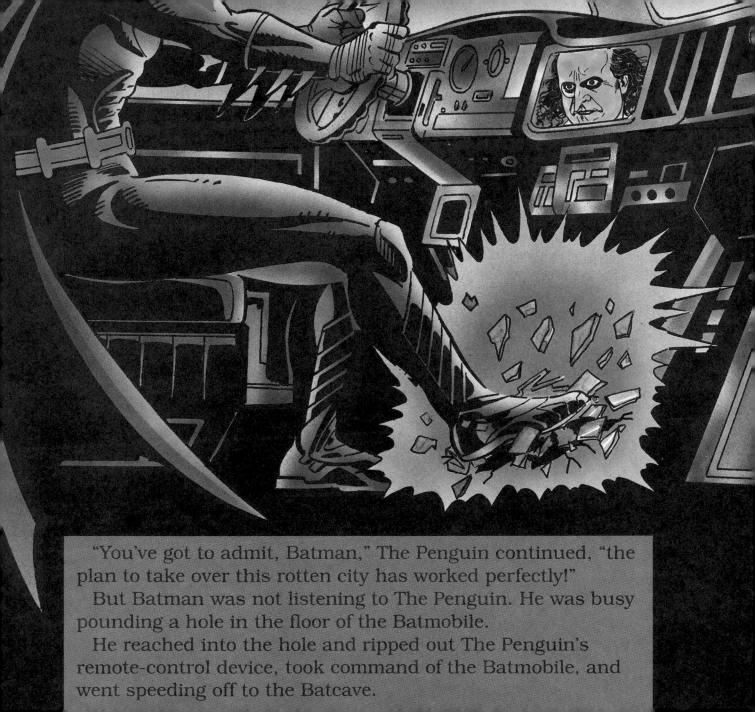

"You've got to admit, Batman," The Penguin continued, "the plan to take over this rotten city has worked perfectly!"

But Batman was not listening to The Penguin. He was busy pounding a hole in the floor of the Batmobile.

He reached into the hole and ripped out The Penguin's remote-control device, took command of the Batmobile, and went speeding off to the Batcave.

The next day The Penguin held a big rally in Gotham Plaza.
While he was speaking, Batman and Alfred were working with
special equipment in the Batcave.

"Are you ready, Alfred?" asked Batman.

"Everything is hooked up, sir," replied Alfred. "We can cut
into the public-address system in the plaza now."

"I hope The Penguin enjoys the sound of his own voice,"
said Batman.

The CD recording played back loud and clear: "It was easy for me to frame you, Batman. . . ."

The Penguin was stunned to hear his own voice coming from the plaza's speakers.

"I didn't say that!" he shouted to the crowd.

But it was too late. The crowd heard The Penguin's words and quickly turned from admiring supporters into an angry mob. The Penguin dashed away and headed for his hideout.

That evening in Wayne Manor, Bruce and Alfred busily trimmed their Christmas tree.

"Fortunately, our little trick with the CD recording outsmarted The Penguin and restored Batman's good name," said Bruce.

"Yes, sir," said Alfred. "It looks like it's going to be a merry Christmas for Gotham City, after all!"

"Indeed it does," replied Bruce, "and a merry Christmas for Batman!"